Rhonda

Bunny Runs Away

by Bernice Chardiet
and Grace Maccarone
pictures by G. Brian Karas

SCHOLASTIC INC.
New York Toronto London Auckland Sydney

In memory of my grandmother, Grazia Maccarone
G.M.

To Edith and Dorothy, my favorite cousins,
and to the childhood we shared at 1883
B.C.

To Tierney
G.B.K.

ISBN 0-590-44932-X

12 11 10 9 8 7 6 5 4 3 2 1 1 2 3 4 5 6/9

Printed in the U.S.A. 08

First Scholastic printing, November 1991

"Coats on!" Ms. Darcy called.

It was almost time to go home.
Bunny was very excited.
Cynthia was coming to her house today!

Sammy and Bunny traded places in line.
Now Bunny stood right in front of Cynthia.

"Where are you going?" Brenda asked Cynthia.
"This isn't the way to your house."
"I know," Cynthia said. "I'm going
to Bunny's house."
Brenda made a face.

Bunny's mother opened the door.
"My mother said she'll get me
at five o'clock," Cynthia said.
"That's fine," said Bunny's mother.

The girls went to play in Bunny's room.
"See what my uncle Peter gave me,"
said Bunny.
It was a brand-new clay set—with smooth
strips of clay in perfect rows of
green, yellow, pink, and blue.

Bunny gave Cynthia the green piece and
the pink piece.
She kept the yellow piece and the blue
piece for herself.

"I don't want pink," Cynthia said.
"I want yellow."
Bunny frowned as she gave Cynthia
the yellow piece.

"Wait!" said Cynthia. "I have to put on my eyeglasses. The doctor said I need them for close work."
Cynthia was very proud of her new glasses. She thought they made her look very smart.

Cynthia made a yellow and green turtle. Bunny made two snakes—a blue one and a pink one.

Bunny rolled her snakes into a ball.
Then she made an elephant.
Cynthia just kept looking at her turtle.
"Why don't you make something else?"
Bunny asked.
"Because I don't want to ruin
my turtle," Cynthia said. "I want
to give it to my father."
"You can't give it to your father,"
Bunny said. "It's my clay!"
"But it's my turtle!" Cynthia yelled.
"No, it's not," said Bunny. "I just
let you play with my clay. You have
to give it back."

Cynthia yelled "No!" and pushed Bunny.

Bunny pushed her back and grabbed the turtle.

Cynthia pulled Bunny's hair.
Bunny tried to grab Cynthia's hair.
Oops! She knocked off Cynthia's glasses.
"You broke my glasses!" Cynthia howled.
"I'm going home!"

"You can't go home," Bunny yelled.
"You have to wait for your mother."
But Cynthia was already out the door.

Bunny's mother heard the door slam.
"What's all the noise about?" she asked.
"Where's Cynthia?"
"She went home," Bunny said.
"We had a fight."

"I'm surprised at you, Bunny," her mother said. "You're not supposed to fight with your guest."

"But she started it," Bunny said.
"She took my clay."
"You should have called me,"
said Bunny's mother.
"I'm going out to find Cynthia.
We'll talk about this when I
get back. In the meantime,
you are to stay in your room."
"That's not fair! You're my mother!
You're supposed to take my side!"
Bunny shouted.

Bunny slammed her door.
"Cynthia was all wrong," Bunny sobbed.
"Mommy cares more about Cynthia than she cares about me. I'm running away!"

Bunny packed her red suitcase with
her pajamas, her toothbrush, and
her favorite doll.

Bunny's eyes blurred with tears
as she waited for the elevator.
She got off on the next floor.

Bunny knocked on the door of
her aunt Betty's apartment.
But no one was home.
Bunny had to wait a long time.

Her cousin Alison came home first.
Alison looked at Bunny's suitcase
and at her red eyes.
"I'm running away," Bunny said.
"Really?" said Alison.
"Where are you going?"
"I don't know yet," said Bunny.
"Then come inside and I'll polish
your nails," said Alison.
"That way you'll look grown-up,
and people won't wonder why
you're all by yourself."

Soon after that, Bunny's cousin Jill came home from ballet class. She was still wearing a leotard and tights.

"Let's dance," Bunny said.
"No. Let's play school," said Jill.

"Can I be the teacher?" Bunny asked.
"No. I'm older than you.
I'm the teacher," Jill said.
"What's twelve times three?"
"That's too hard," said Bunny.
"What's twelve times two?" said Jill.
"I don't know," Bunny said.

JILL
A+
JILL
A+
JILL
A+
12 x 3
12 x 2

"Then you have to sit in the
dummy corner," Jill said.
"No, I won't," Bunny shouted.
"We don't have a dummy corner
in Ms. Darcy's class."
"Well, we do in *my* class," Jill said.

"Well, I'm not in *your* class anymore," Bunny said. "I'm leaving. Right now!"

Aunt Betty came in from shopping.
"Bunny, what are you doing here?
Your mother is looking all over
for you!"
"I'm running away from home,"
Bunny said.
"Oh, dear," said her aunt.
"Your mother will be so sorry.
And so will we."

Bunny began to cry.
She didn't want to run away anymore.
Bunny wanted her mother.
Just then someone knocked on the door.

It was Bunny's mother.
"I still can't find Bunny!"
she said.

Bunny ran to her mother and gave her
a big hug.
"Here I am," Bunny said. "I ran away.
But I'm coming back. I missed you."
"I missed you, too," Bunny's mother
said. "But why did you run away?"
"I thought you liked Cynthia better
than me. I thought you didn't love me
anymore," said Bunny.
Bunny's mother hugged Bunny back.
"I could never stop loving you,"
she said.

"Would you like to stay for dinner?" Aunt Betty asked. "We're having fish."
"No, thank you," said Bunny's mother. "We're going to have a very special dinner because Bunny is coming home. We'll have all her favorites."
"Even chocolate pudding?" Bunny asked.
"Even chocolate pudding," said her mother.

Bunny and her mother held hands as they went back to their apartment.

That night Cynthia called.
"My mother fixed my eyeglasses,"
Cynthia said. "I'm sorry I tried
to take your clay. Do you want to
come over to my house tomorrow?"

"Yes," said Bunny. "We can play school.
We can take turns being Ms. Darcy."